For Franny

I wrote most of this and so much more with you curled up nearby, purring away. Now that you're gone I can still hear that little motor. Sleep well, kitty.

ACEGIKMOQSUWY

Gesamtkunstwerk!

The following is a work of fiction. All events, characters, and places (including Paris, France) are entirely fictional and in no way, shape, or form represent anything that has ever been real for any duration of time. For example, the character Gertrude Stein featured in this story, based on the modernist poet Gertrude Stein, does not represent any Gertrude Steins living or dead. She is simply words on a page and a construct of your imagination. Essentially she represents the Gertrude Stein in all of us. But also none of us because she doesn't exist. If you do happen to have an actual Gertrude Stein within you it is advised you seek out immediate medical attention. That is unless your name happens to be Gertrude Stein and the Gertrude Stein within you is yourself. That is perfectly normal and provided you are feeling well no medical attention is required. Also keep in mind that the character Gertrude Stein featured in this story, based on the actual modernist poet Gertrude Stein, is an entirely fictitious Gertrude Stein and not you. Even if you happen to be a modernist poet named Gertrude Stein and the events of this story resemble the events of your life exactly, it is entirely coincidental and the following story is not meant to be a depiction of you or your life but rather is a work of fiction. It is not real. Just like everything discussed in this story, especially Paris, France, is not real. It can't even be proven that you, this book, or that dog barking outside are real. Was there a dog barking outside as you read that line? What are the odds?

ZXVTRPNLJHFDCB

—
—

三

1

Tender Buttons Two:
Disco Wreck Lord

A novelette or Short Story or Anthology
or Whatever. Does it really matter?
Is it hurting anyone if we don't define it
as one thing or another? It's a cantaloupe,
okay? Let's just call it a f'n cantaloupe.

* * *

by Keith Blenman

Blue Donut Books
ISBN: 978-0-9890234-4-3

Chapter 4

"Darling? My darling? Is that you? Why did you never come home?"

The grammar police of old Scotland Yard had their hands full with some American in Paris. What had started as a simple display of expressionism soon broke into full speed Dadaist cubism and spiraled beyond what anybody -let alone any European- could've proclaimed as *controlled*.

"It's unlike anything I've ever witnessed before," Jenkins told The Chief Inspector, trotting along his motorcar as it came to a halt. He opened the door with all the urgency their situation demanded and gave a grateful salute. Finally, he thought. Order would be restored.

The Chief Inspector, his steel grey eyes, regarded Jenkins with a small salute and even smaller nod. The constable's words meant little in context as Jenkins was only a stock character and not developed enough to have seen much of interest. Still, now was hardly the time for whiting out the rookies. The Chief Inspector had a bigger meal on his plate. Stepping from the rear passenger door of his motorcar, he adjusted his custodian helmet and asked, "What is it then? Don't tell me I left the office over a trifle of typos or some philanderer making rash abuses of double entendres again."

"Nothing so miniscule, sir," Jenkins said, shutting the door, saluting the driver, and then dashing to meet The Chief Inspector on his way to the command station. "It's a full on hostage situation in there. A modernist, we think but the structure's gone batsy. Everything's ineligible."

The Chief Inspector's moustache twitched. He stopped, violently turning to Jenkins. It seemed he had a moment to white out a rookie after all.

"Illegible, sir!" Jenkins corrected himself. "Sorry, sir. Slip of the tongue, sir."

The Chief Inspector let the rookie's words hang in his throat a moment before asking, "Batsy?"

Jenkins lower lip trembled. He'd never used the non-word before. He couldn't place where he'd learned it. Under the Inspector's commanding glare he probably also couldn't recall his own shoe size. Had his middle name been requested in the moment it likely would've been conveyed through an uncertain stutter. He was embarrassed and his anxieties shook him enough to rattle the cobblestones he stood upon.

"Relax, constable," The Chief Inspector said coolly. "All the new recruits get tangled up when they try whipping out their big dictionaries. Nothing to be embarrassed over. Nothing to be promoted over either, but one day at a time." He didn't dignify his joke with a smile or even a squint. It made the rookie squirm and The Chief Inspector enjoyed watching him twist. Men forced into knots learned rigidity.

They reached the command center and The Chief Inspector let Jenkins open the door for him. It was a wide enough trailer, but a little too French for his tastes. Several other officers were busy thumbing through reference books and jotting copious notes. "What's it today, gentlemen?" The Chief Inspector spoke casually but was met with pale faces and vacant stares.

"It's…" Millieu, a PhD from the Hamptons stuttered. "It's absurdist. The writing on the wall is the wall and walled off but the wall must come down."

Everybody froze and turned to Millieu.

A trickle of sweat greased the PhD's face. "The walls between us are defined!" he said, bringing a hand to his own mouth in a gasp. "The walls between us are the walls between all men but unique to us." He shook his head and bit his lower lip. Looking around frantically, Millieu stammered and leapt from his chair, backing into a corner. "The walls have holes and semi permeable pores but never forget themselves as walls!" He screamed and slapped himself. "The walls are built and rebuilt over a lifetime because our fathers built their walls after our grandfathers' walls! The walls must fall but they're too thick because building walls was all our fathers taught us!"

"Calm yourself, man!" The Chief Inspector dashed through his agape troops and grabbed Millieu by the wrists, just before the man could take a red pen to himself. "Calm down! You're fixated on an image. Get off it!"

Millieu burst into tears as he said, "A wall is a symbol of a wall is a symbol of a symbol of a wall!"

The Chief Inspector had heard enough. He gave Millieu a quick crack to the temple and eased the PhD's unconscious body to the floor. He'd seen rookies and even a sergeant collapse under pressure, but never a seasoned man like Millieu. He was a studied, skilled editor and the force had been privileged for his many contributions. He'd been around the block thrice and seen more than men twice his years. From second grade spelling contests to sci-fi fan fiction, nothing shook Millieu. And there he was, cracking under the pressure like some kid who'd misused a semicolon. "What in the devil happened to this man?"

One of the other officers piped in, "He was just sitting there. He'd been rambling about taking his daughter and nieces on a holiday. I gave him only a single abstract to start. *The white hunter is nearly crazy*. It had a title too. *The White Hunter*."

"Is that all? What of the rest of the passage? Did it say anything on walls?"

The officer fell silent.

"Well?"

"That's just the thing, sir. *The White Hunter. The white hunter is nearly crazy.* That was the entirety of it."

The chief inspector looked between the officer and Millieu. He didn't understand. He couldn't understand. Someone gave a title to a single sentence? "How long had he been working it?"

"Not ten minutes, sir. He arrived shortly before you. But…" the officer trailed off, trying to find rationality for his own words. "He's the fifth man, sir. The fifth driven mad."

"What have you people been reading?"

"Stein, sir," Jenkins chimed in from over The Chief Inspector's shoulder. "The author's name is Gertrude Stein."

Chapter 4

The Chief Inspector's name wasn't James, John, Patrick, Peter, William, or most of the others. He wasn't single or any longer wed and the subject often reminded him of his bereavement. He'd been a father for only a moment and never given the chance to be a dad. He wasn't a slight man, nor stocky. His most intimidating feature was his gaze. He'd earned it over a lifetime and it showed. He looked at everyone like he'd seen them naked, weeping, with their hands stuck in the rear of a piggy bank. Nobody thought him a cruel man. Nobody found him judgmental. His uniform could be filled with any manner of metals, ribbons, stars, or the sort of recognitions that came dangled with fringe. But he adorned it only with his badge because that was the one thing people needed to know of him. He could do his job. If asked the sort of fellow he'd become, his peers always deferred to his pistol.

The gun gleamed silver. It wasn't fancy or ornamental. It had been made to function and it did that well. It had been used at range and it had been used as a club. Wear showed mostly in the handle but nobody doubted its sturdiness. It was a Smith & Wesson revolver with too much kick for one hand, but that's exactly how The Chief Inspector fired it. He'd carried it since his days in the service, but the pages of how he'd acquired it had long since been blacked out, shredded, and left to warm in a furnace. People thought he'd stop carrying it once he joined the grammar police but he hadn't. Nowadays they all supposed it'd only be proper to bury him with it. Nobody knew his wishes and nobody asked. All anybody could say for sure was that if the Chief Inspector pulled his gun, something was about to end.

He called it Mittens.

Gertrude Stein's Dossier:
Not Chapter 4

The mug shots were made from recycled ink donated by the love child of Dali and Picasso and painted with Van Gogh's ear. It was less cruel than harming a sable, ox, pony, squirrel, hog, or another sable. Asparagus is linear not as linear near in its peak but pointed and a life on paper can never summarize a life. There was sweetness in the brother's remark of abomination but people with money don't always have manors and being sweeter than English is simpler on a canvas that can't be read.

Gertrude Stein was a woman. Gertrude Stein was a writer. Gertrude Stein had time, money, and power and made or bought history as she saw fit but we don't know which and never ever never once did it show in her mug shots. The man who made her mug shots wasn't sure if *mug shot* was one word or two. The record never once considers whether or knotted not she liked frogs. The record doesn't show that women have all the power and are the species constant and men are a grapefruit powerless function acting out as variables with different values exceeding their numeration in an effort to make those with power dependent upon them in spite of the fact that they are Y and women are X. The record nearly forgot how she is the reason we have our literature and only the smallest circles discuss her in school. The record knows her associates but isn't big enough for history. The Chinese diplomat in Greece doesn't require the record.

The record doesn't show that a man of grammar can't overpower a woman enabled to dance around it. It doesn't know whether or not a man can survive because although it's written and the trajectories were established long before the record was written, it can't be recorded until it's been interpreted. The woman died in 1946 –three years after Maude Dunn- and the man never existed and doesn't know he's only a man because Y is its most interesting when defined by X.

———
— —

Chapter 4

The Chief Inspector held up his bullhorn. "All right, Stein! You had your fun. Now let the English go!" He stared from the cobblestone street to the mansion and he hated the mansion. It was just another useless spectacle full of objects, food, and rooms. Boxes within a box, each with a purpose but none more so than to satisfy their owner's ego. A man could lose himself in a mansion. Many more lost or gave up on themselves on the road toward one. Not that he was any sort of socialist, communist, or had a type of ethos anyone could call into question. He just knew the mansion wasn't worth what it symbolized.

The Chief Inspector sighed. He'd been here too long already. He was starting to sound like Millieu. "You hear me in there, Stein? A lot of good men out here are going away in white jackets. You've caused quite a stir."

The lights in the mansion began to flicker. The blinds breathed and the shutters asynchronously oscillated. Gertrude Stein's highly distinct voice was then imagined in saying, "A white jacket is a seagull beak slapping the shore. Otters odder utter lift bellies was the way we danced on tiptoes patiently. Andy was after Toby and Y stands outside because why asks the people. Everything sacred meant to be devoured milked bled until the husk is fertilized in proper green black becomes the swan. We eat the swan, sir. And then we eat the swan."

The Chief Inspector's moustache twitched. Once. He slowly turned to Jenkins, and Jenkins could only shake his head. He turned back to the mansion, knowing that behind him three more pairs of men in white were hauling away his cackling officers on stretchers. Several of the old squad cars were ablaze, seemingly because that was just the sort of thing that would be happening in a moment such as this. The chief inspector felt their warmth on his shoulders. He closed his eyes and for nearly two seconds remembered lifting his wife's veil on their wedding day so many summers ago. With a long, audible sigh he lifted the bullhorn and his eyes. To Getrude Stein he said, "Everything sacred *is* meant to be devoured. *It is* milked *and* bled until the husk is *properly* fertilized. Now let my people go."

The mansion was silent. Its lights didn't flicker. The shutters weren't in motion. From the chimney, several bubbles of smoke plumed out.

Jenkins, for no particular purpose other than an inability to maintain composure, took a half step forward. "Did that work?" he said. "Just correcting her, sir. Was that all that was needed?"

The Chief Inspector didn't answer. Had this been war, Jenkins would've taken a bullet six times over by now. It was amazing the constable hadn't gone mad or turned in his badge yet. For that he had to be given some credit. Some. Not-

The street rumbled. A pulse. A thundering ring spread from the mansion, rattling its lawn, the landscaping, and the cobblestone at the officer's feet. As it spread, the shingles slid from neighboring rooftops. And just as all the men regained their balance the ring constricted back in.

Every light in the mansion flooded the streets. All the blinds blew out as every shutter slapped the exterior walls. Gertrude's voice blared well out of the city and into the countryside. "A need is a handed over thread straw grasped finally to insist a spooling un-ended. Ants don their tomorrow in rows with steps every all not knowing the millions ahead. The serve is volleyed. The game is played until it isn't. The game is playing the game. We were are never here but something felt unclosed a book prevented. A need doesn't have to be basic to be needed. A need is needed occasional thus virtue of because she or he or he couldn't calculate to say *require*."

By the time Stein finished all the officers had to pick themselves up off the rumbling roads and dust themselves off. All except for The Chief Inspector. He alone stood his ground. It wasn't until the lights began to dim that he lifted his bullhorn and said, "A need is a something required due to importance. Ants carry food on their backs. And we're here because you're defiling language. Plain and simple."

The shutters, lights, and cobblestones all spasmed. "A language is a smack of jellyfish and conformity of hipsters. The shape is the made up unmade up writhing sanded slathered twice to finite corners. Indefinitely in a boxed out box. A rose is a rose is a rose is a whale of a whale of a bowl of petunias. A sunset is synchronization. But you saw color not why color but my green is three shades deeper over over an ocean knowing. Sunsets aren't born or swallowed when oceans are marbled. Licorice twists when it's makes but not told to but extruders are made to tell to twist. No one defines the moment yet happened. Spaghetti slurps smacks the face spot of its choosing in death rattle revenge. America means more words than Americas agree and fewer and more in Italy. The cat runs crawl on smooth floors. Frenzied fulminating is the marble and language is crock pot cookery."

There it was. The Chief Inspector felt Stein's symbolism the moment it happened. Even in extremes, even in a violent Dadaist escapism the artist still needed rules to break. Some rules would be her focus. Some she'd conform to automatically. That's where he'd find her and that's where he'd beat her. The last thing she said. The poetics. The craft. There was art to her work, and for that he had the upper hand.

The lights flickered. "An upper hand is best clandestine," Stein said as the thought rolled through The Chief Inspector. "A broken thing echoes its discontinuation. Lydia screamed and died in agony. Caleb never tasted enough air to scream."

The handle of the bullhorn shattered in The Chief Inspector's fist. "Enough banter," he said to Jenkins, dropping the bullhorn and letting the useless tool shatter against the street. "We're breaching the mansion."

"Sir?" Jenkins said as his knees buckled. He stared at his superior's white hot eyes and twitching moustache.

"Get Officer Strunk and Agent White," The Chief Inspector said, turning sharply back to the command center. "We're breaching."

Chapter Swathe:
The Legality of Choice

Jenkins was not quite a teenager again, sitting at a campfire at the edge of a deforested stump field with his father, George Washington, Nikola Tesla, and Edgar Allen Poe. A red sun was humbling itself to the horizon and all the men were smoking their pipes in safari wear while cleaning rifles and casually tending to ballpark franks as they roasted over the fire. Jenkins whittled away at a chunk of weak stone, forming the shape of a falcon claw until his father looked upon it disapprovingly and threw it into the fire. There was a somber silence between the man and his son that carried for a long crackling moment until Jenkins father returned his attention to the rest of his hunting party and asked, "Have I ever told you gents about the time I was raped by a fruit bat?"

Tesla gulped from a beer stein and said, "I'm sorry. Did you say you were bound and gagged by an elk?"

"No, no," Jenkins' father said. "But the history books may as well say as much."

George Washington slouched his back to the words *history* and *books*. "I was perhaps a dozen or so men over the course of my life," he said. "History has written me as one, and not all of me true."

Edgar Allen Poe made no remark to this, but had any of the other men or the boy bothered to look in his eyes, they would've seen the deepest parts of his soul weeping openly before them.

"Gentlemen! Gentlemen!" Jenkins' father said stamping his beer down on a log he'd chopped down himself earlier that day. "We're losing ourselves here. I was of course about to regale you all with an anecdote from my years spent in Brazil. That's Brazil, South America mind you. Not Africa. But I certainly saw my share of hunting there as well. Now, the exact events of the story don't matter as long as the feeling of it is clear. The overall point of my tale is simply that I underwent some unfortunate happenstance of which I am no longer burdened to endure. Be it being bound by elk, bamboozled by iguanas, or –as I was saying- raped by a fruit bat. Your take-away is the emotion and newfound perspective."

"Father," Jenkins sighed pitifully in a pastel blue sailor suit his mother had elected he wear to impress the gentlemen. It clashed with the rainbow colored lollipop he held limply in his left hand. "Father," he said. "They don't want to hear the fruit bat story."

Jenkins' father slapped him clean across the face, knocking the lollipop to the ground. "Of course they want to hear the fruit bat story! Everybody wants to hear the blasted fruit bat story! They're mortified over bats. And a raping will certainly turn some stomachs. But the hook of it reels in listeners because of its absurdity! The fact of the fact of the fact is that nobody looks away when something unspeakable happens right in front of them. Nobody!"

Jenkins lower lip trembled. He watched as a small army of ants gathered around his lollipop, lifted it together, and carried it off toward the valley.

"So there I was, armed with nothing but my trusty blunderbuss, hunting wild cats close range through the rain forest. When all of a sudden, right over my left shoulder I hear this determined little voice squeaking all manner of absurdities at me. I glance over myself and the creature hisses at my face while grinding its way hard against my shoulder blade. Stupid, blind little creature missed every orifice on my body and thank God for it. Of course I was puzzled by the thing at first. I knew full well its intention but the audacity of its boldness struck me sour. I wasn't having it. No sir! Regardless of creed or species, that was not something I was about to accept. And I wanted to make sure all the blasted creatures of the forest knew not to try such funny business with me again. For I am a man. And I am the most dominant of God's creations. No other animal would ever take that away from me. So I took myself a nice, slow puff of my cigar, letting the animal think it'd receive no retaliation for its offense, and then aimed my blunderbuss through my own shoulder. One trigger pull was all it took. One trigger pull and no bat, wasp, hare, nor bear has ever again considered to un-manifest my destiny. Of course I wasn't out of the woods –heh- just yet."

Jenkins stopped listening to his father entirely. He'd heard the story a billion times before. His father stopped the bleeding with cigar burns. The natives of the local village carved him a new arm, the same arm he wears to this day. It was always the same old story. For the millionth time. Yet again. Man gets sexually assaulted by a bat. Man shoots off his own shoulder. Man returns to his real America, ever the conquering hero. Jenkins was bored of the paradigm. He just sighed to himself and watched his lollipop reach a hole at the top of an anthill. The ants stuck the tip of the stick into the hole and slowly lowered it in. It was stopped of course by the enormous candy circle at the top of the stick, but that didn't seem to slow the ants ambition. They lifted the lollipop stick slightly from the hole and tried plunging it down again. And again. And again. As they repeatedly failed the stick was lifted and lowered more rapidly, the candy lollipop being rammed repeatedly into the earth, the ants doing all they could to breach the surface.

Poe finally had enough. "That is quite possibly the single worst story I've ever had unfolded before me in all my life," he said.

Tesla downed the foam from his empty beer stein. "Well I found it rather lovely," he said.

The fortune to be divided.
Two quarters into the trust and scholarships.
The other half between the children
but divided into thirds.
To Phyllis, Eliza, and Pierre,
A fifth-billion each.
Six butterscotches to Roderick.

Chapter 38:
Parallels

The Chief Inspector passed the butters in your local grocery market. He stared passively at the lot of them. Sticks. Tubs. Salted. Unsalted. Reduced fat. Reduced butter. Unprocessed. Twice-processed. He remembered his childhood on the farm. He remembered his father teaching him to milk cows and churn his own butter. There was something beautiful about the simple things. Tall grass fields. Happy cattle. Maybe if the war had never come he'd have grown to be a different man.

An elderly woman passed on his left, lightly bumping his hand with the side of her grocery cart. "Do you need a psychiatrist?[1]" she said, smiling apologetically at him.

"Pardon me?" The Chief Inspector said.

"Do you need a psychiatrist?[2]" The elderly woman said, pointing to his hand. "Do you need a psychiatrist?[3]"

The Chief Inspector blinked several times, regarding the woman. "I'm fine," he said. "Thank you."

The woman nodded, embarrassment clearly in her eyes, but she continued passing him before reaching for a small tub of Junior John John's Butter *Lite*. The chief inspector watched her, puzzled over such a peculiar question. He chocked it up to nothing. Just a random little happenstance to regale to his wife and son's graves on Sunday. The old woman set the butter down in the child seat of her shopping basket, gave him one final smile, and walked off to the next item on her shopping list.

---

[1] "Oh. Excuse me, sir."

[2] "Did I hurt you?"

[3] "Are you all right?"

The Chief Inspector returned his attention to the wall of butter, although memories of his father had passed and he decided to move on. He pushed a grocery cart down the aisle until he reached the milk. There he saw half percent, two percent, skim, and eggnog. But not the whole milk. Not the staple milk of his entire life, the milk he identified with breakfast and an occasional evening cocoa in winter. He stepped back from the cooler to get a broader view. When he was certain he didn't see it he leaned forward to start inspecting for different colored caps among the rows of milk gallons. Among them all there wasn't a single gallon of whole milk to be had. The Chief Inspector sighed. He supposed some two percent would do but it was rather odd for your grocery market to be lacking stock of such a thing. The Chief Inspector looked around. A young lady in the uniform you're used to seeing on the employees in your local grocery market was slapping a price gun to assorted boxes of cheese. "Excuse me," The Chief Inspector said to her. "Excuse me, young miss?"

The young lady looked up and smiled at The Chief Inspector. "Do you need a psychiatrist?[4]" she said.

The Chief Inspector chuckled. The young lady must've heard the elderly woman talking to him. "Perhaps," he joked. "There doesn't seem to be any whole milk. Would you mind checking in the back for a gallon?"

The young lady nodded and set down her pricing gun. She said, "Do you need psychiatrist?[5]" and trotted off.

The Chief Inspector watched the young lady head down the aisle and step through the doors you typically see leading to employee only areas of your local grocery market. She had seemed compliant enough but to repeat the joke without any indication of humor was off putting. He looked back to the milks, studying their many white gallons, each with labels identical to those you're used to seeing on milk gallons. For all their comfort and familiarity, he felt himself becoming unsettled. He looked around the grocery market. He saw people shopping. Employees going about their work. It was busy enough but didn't feel crowded.

A middle-aged man approached from behind him. "Do you need a psychiatrist?[6]" he said, pointing generally to all the milk.

---

[4] "Hello, sir. Can I help you?"

[5] "Of course! I'll be right back."

[6] "Mind if I squeeze by? I just need a gallon of milk."

The Chief Inspector lightly slapped the handlebar of his shopping basket. He said, "Is this some game?" staring the man square in the eyes.

The man froze and stared at The Chief Inspector, giving back the same uncomfortable stare so many rookies had given him in the past. It was giving The Chief Inspector a headache, mostly because it reminded him of Jenkins. The man was slack jawed for a moment, but after a short gulp he said, "Do you need a psychiatrist?[7]"

The Chief Inspector's hands tightened against the cart as he said, "No, I don't need a bloody psychiatrist!"

The man stood up a little straighter and took a step backwards. "Do you need a psychiatrist?[8]" he said, his eyes growing wide with fear. As The Chief Inspector took a step toward him he stumbled and said, "Do you need a psychiatrist?[9]" before regaining his balance and running off to another aisle.

The Chief Inspector watched him run for only a moment. He noticed other people were beginning to stare. "Bloody creep," he said to them, gesturing at the customer as he rounded the corner.

One of the other patrons, some buff kid snorted. "Do you need a psychiatrist?[10]" he said, making the same gesture back at The Chief Inspector.

A mother with two children seemed to agree. "Do you need a psychiatrist?[11]" she said.

"What's the ploy here?" The Chief Inspector said, his face turning red as people began to circle. "Why do you all keep saying that?"

"Do you need a psychiatrist?[12]" an old man said.

---

[7] "No. I just need some milk."

[8] "Look, mister. I don't want any trouble."

[9] "I'll come back another time!"

[10] "You're the one being a creep, man."

[11] "Yeah, why don't you get lost?"

[12] "Saying what?"

He was followed by a middle-aged woman with saggy eyes and a mole on her forehead who asserted herself with, "Do you need a psychiatrist?[13]" This was followed by another employee who put up his arms and said to everybody, "Do you need a psychiatrist?[14]"

As the people gathered and closed in, The Chief Inspector instinctively reached for his pistol. "Stop saying that," he said. "Everybody stop speaking right now." His fingertips grazed the suede leather holster.

The employee continued with his hands up. "Do you need a psychiatrist?[15]" he said. "Do you need a psychiatrist?[16]"

"Do you need a psychiatrist?[17]" the young lady returned holding a half-gallon of milk in both hands. The cap was the color you're used to seeing with whole milk. Shuffling her way through the crowd the young lady said, "Do you need a psychiatrist?[18]"

The Chief Inspector eyed the milk. Whatever it was that was going on at your local grocery market, he had had enough. He stepped toward the girl and snatched the half-gallon from her. "Just leave me alone!" he screamed at the crowd, turning abruptly away. "Stop speaking to me!"

The young lady sneered at the Chief Inspector. "Do you need a psychiatrist?[19]" she said.

---

[13] "Because you're being a creep, you psycho! Why didn't you just let that poor man get his milk?"

[14] "All right, everyone calm down. There's no reason to raise your voices."

[15] "It's all right, sir. Just calm down. There's no reason to be upset."

[16] "Is there anything I can help you with?"

[17] "I've got it, Trevor."

[18] "We didn't have any gallons but I found a half gallon. Is that okay?"

[19] "You're welcome. Asshole."

The Chief Inspector looked over his shoulder at her. "Stop that!" he snapped, losing himself and tripping over his own foot. He fell face first, the half gallon breaking his fall and bursting beneath him. Just as quickly as he fell he tried to stand but slipped through the white puddle on the tile floor and fell again. Embarrassed, broken, he remained there.

Everybody, employees and patrons alike, gathered around as The Chief Inspector exhaled a long, calming breath. The young lady shook her head. "Do you need a psychiatrist?[20]" she sighed.

---

[20] "You need a psychiatrist."

Intermission

Swindled by a stranger's charm, I cast three seeds aimlessly on the lawn last night. I'd jested a beanstalk but to my surprise at sunrise I saw myself gestating from the vines. Three me's of near equal size, but only one breathing. "What are you?" I asked myself in a whisper, and then the other I answered.

"Cold."

Of his kind, the second sprouted funny and lied lifeless with his head still in the dirt. The third it seemed choked on the vine of the first, leaving it dry, wilted, and unable to ripen.

I draped the first in a frost cloth and it asked for water.

"From the hose or a glass?"

"A pot," he said. "One large enough to fit your- err, my head."

Chapters
23 5 12 12,
20 8 1 20
23 1 19
19 20 (19-1) 1 14 7 5.

Agent White ran up a proverb and leapt to the nearest haiku. Swinging his red pen he crossed out six paraphrases and kicked the personification of personification square in the motif.

"Ha-haa!" Officer Strunk saluted Agent White before correcting a typo. He dashed along a run-on sentence, threw himself through excessively repeated words, ducked beneath questionable italics, sprang from some underlined vocabulary, and circled a misused semi-colon with every last fiber of his being. Just as he thought he could take a breath he saw an explanation point following a question mark at the end of a fragment. "My god," he said, reaching for the white-out.

White saw the over-punctuation and was about to join his partner but was stopped when he came under a barrage of hyphenation. He juked betwixt the words before they connected. He performed several flips and an aerial until he reached the end of a sentence and leapt (and/or leaped) upon a paragraph of heavy exposition.

This cavalier use of language was formidable for both White and Strunk but hardly anything they hadn't seen before. The duo had met in the forties whilst investigating a children's national spelling bee that served as a front in the Portuguese slang trade. Their back-story became the basis of the second revised classical paradigm. Their continued adventures developed into the inspiration for grammar and reference books everywhere. Also tales along the lines of *Beowulf* and *The Count of Monte Cristo*. Even though they were written centuries prior, Strunk and White's pure awesomeness transcended time.

The two stood back to back, crossing out and correcting a horde of ambiguous anecdotes. Strunk scribbled *be specific* to compliment White's *unclear*. And yet the tactfully poor writing poured a continuous stream of adverbs and sentences ending in prepositions.

"What is this madness?" White said from beneath his ninja mask. Also, he was wearing a ninja mask.

"Another notch in the belt," Strunk said, a playful smirk on his lips as he sharpened a red pencil. "Quick! Cover that alliteration!"

Chapter Red Door

RED DOOR RED DOOR RED DOOR RED DOOR RED DOOR RED
DOOR RED DOOR RED DOOR RED DOOR RED DOOR RED
DOOR RED DOOR RED DOOR RED DOOR RED DOOR RED
DOOR RED DOOR RED DOOR RED DOOR RED DOOR RED
DOOR RED DOOR RED DOOR RED DOOR RED DOOR RED
DOOR RED DOOR RED DOOR RED DOOR RED DOOR RED
DOOR RED DOOR RED DOOR RED DOOR RED DOOR RED
DOOR RED DOOR RED DOOR RED DOOR RED DOOR RED
DOOR RED DOOR RED DOOR RED DOOR RED DOOR RED
DOOR RED DOOR RED DOOR RED DOOR RED DOOR RED
DOOR RED DOOR RED DOOR RED DOOR RED DOOR RED
DOOR RED DOOR ROD DEER RED DOOR RED DOOR RED
DOOR RED DOOR RED DOOR RED DOOR RED DOOR RED
DOOR RED DOOR RED DOOR RED DOOR RED DOOR RED
DOOR RED DOOR RED DOOR RED DOOR RED DOOR RED
DOOR RED DOOR RED DOOR RED DOOR RED DOOR RED
DOOR RED DOOR RED DOOR RED DOOR RED DOOR RED
DOOR RED DOOR RED DOOR RED DOOR RED DOOR RED
DOOR RED DOOR RED DOOR RED DOOR RED DOOR RED
DOOR RED DOOR RED DOOR RED DOOR RED DOOR RED
DOOR RED DOOR RED DOOR RED DOOR RED DOOR RED
DOOR RED DOOR RED DOOR RED DOOR RED DOOR RED
DOOR RED DOOR RED DOOR RED DOOR RED DOOR RED
DOOR RED DOOR RED DOOR RED DOOR DER ROOD RED
DOOR RED DOOR RED DOOR RED DOOR RED DOOR RED
DOOR RED DOOR RED DOOR RED DOOR RED DOOR RED
DOOR RED DOOR RED DOOR RED DOOR RED DOOR RED
DOOR RED DOOR RED DOOR RED DOOR RED DOOR RED
DOOR RED DOOR RED DOOR RED DOOR RED DOOR RED
DOOR RED DOOR RED DOOR RED DOOR RED DOOR RED
DOOR RED DOOR RED DOOR RED DOOR RED DOOR RED
DOOR RED DOOR RED DOOR RED DOOR RED DOOR RED
DOOR RED DOOR RED DOOR RED DOOR RED DOOR RED
DOOR RED DOOR RED DOOR RED DOOR RED DOOR RED
DOOR RED DOOR RED DOOR RED DOOR RED DOOR RED
DOOR RED DOOR RED DOOR RED DOOR RED DOOR RED
DOOR RED DOOR RED DOOR RED DOOR RED DOOR RED
DOOR RED DOOR RED DOOR.

Proposition 33, Section C.7.2

Stein levitated   the floor because sitting on the
dusty, warped wood caused it to creak with her   motion.
She considered The   Inspector and his band of   ,
unsure of how to categorize them. Flies on her   . Elephants in
her rooms. Warped clocks on her branches. She found her
setting a   dramatic. The highest belfry in a mansion of her
, her positioned as a villain or more honestly a   . She'd
have rather been a   in an editorial about modernism in
the beginning of the   century. This… This couldn't
even be called a   or tragedy. It was something she
but wouldn't have articulated herself. The   structure
and unfiltered   was shameful. This needed a narrative.
This lacked   .

The part of Stein that was Gertrude reflected over the
part of the Inspector that was Chief. He was as is less than a
but more of a   . She pondered his   .

Chapter Bad Diet, Smoker

Carter stood over his corpse and sighed. Three minutes. He supposed he should be proud. He should be relishing this moment. He'd spent three hundred and fourteen lifetimes spinning circles around the universe, ripped through two black holes' event horizons at once, and just this moment proved his theory that the same matter could occupy two spaces simultaneously because A) in the grandeur of existence such miniscule events were entirely irrelevant to the space time continuum and B) the body was constantly shedding and replacing new cells so very little of him was in fact the same matter. He should be tickled over this. He was right and all of existence carried forward. But he was disappointed. When he'd seen himself he screamed. His scream. That shrilly little yelp. No wonder nobody ever took him seriously. And then that fight? He was a slapper. He'd defended himself in a flurry of terrified slaps and took his stabbings like a child. Seeing himself from this side didn't make him feel right about the murder. Or suicide? Quite the contrary. It was sinking in just how little he'd robbed the world of. But he supposed that's why he was here. This time he'd get it right. And he'd start with karate classes. And voice lessons for his screaming. If anybody taught such a thing. He'd find out. Two minutes.

T-Minus One Minute

The Chief Inspector, Jenkins, White, and Strunk all dashed from separate rooms and slammed the doors shut behind them. They pointed red pens, pencils, and white out at each other in a stand off. All it would take is one wrong verb for the men to unleash an over corrective frenzy on each other. That is if they were indeed each other. Jenkins was in a sailor outfit, which raised more than one eyebrow. "What is this place?" he asked, looking at his three superiors, red pencil held high. "Who am I kidding? I don't have any of your eyes or experience." He holstered his red pen and put up his hands.

"Right," The Chief Inspector said, his gaze moving from Strunk to White. "That's definitely Jenkins, backing down from a fight. As for you two, should I have any doubts?"

Strunk said, "If your every sentence admits a doubt, your writing will lack authority."

White nodded to Strunk and said, "A lack of authority is like a weak tummy."

"Don't say 'tummy,'" Strunk said. "Not without good reason." He then lowered his white out and Strunk lowered his pen.

They all looked to The Chief Inspector, who lowered his pen and white out. He was in charge. He'd always be the last to stand down. But with one situation dissolved it was time to move onto the next. "So what are we looking at here?" he asked. "All of you, report."

White was the first to step forward. "In that room were mass nouns functioning as count nouns. I couldn't make sense of its syntax and ended up crossing out paragraphs of dribble. But the corrections were all wrong, each of them making less sense than the words I started my analysis with. Before I knew it the lines were auto-correcting themselves. Soon there wasn't a hint of language to be had and I was being chased by a tsunami of Japanese particles. Had that door not appeared I'd be drowning in high school level French for sure."

Strunk pat his comrade on the shoulder. "My situation was no better. There were linguists, sir. Linguists everywhere. They were devolving event semantics into subatomic structures with second hand first order logic. The lot of them were redefining the significance of grammar laws based on the height of whoever wrote them. All their skin was made of eggshells. When the fighting broke out... They were so fragile. All of them. The yolk, sir. The yolk was everywhere."

The Chief Inspector's wife then said, "Darling? My darling? Is that you?"

The Chief Inspector stared at the furthest wall. "Lydia?" he said.

Jenkins, Strunk, and White all looked to their commanding officer. "Sir?" one of them asked.

The Chief Inspector looked to Jenkins, although he may not have been the one who addressed him. "What's the hold up, Jenkins? Report. What are you doing in that ridiculous outfit?"

Jenkins became nervous under the Chief Inspector's gaze. "I was with my father," he said. "I... I... I haven't the words."

The lights flickered and Gertrude Stein's voice echoed through the hall. "A word is worth a thousand pictures pictures itchers itchers preachers."

"That's enough!" The Chief Inspector snapped at the empty spaces between the walls. "If you think we'll stand for your defilement of syntax then you're gravely mistaken. You hear me, Stein? You're only making matters worse for yourself!"

"You're only making matters I hear mistaken graves defiled enough for syntax," Stein started to say but was melded and finished by Jenkins. All the men turned to the rookie, his typical anxious expression all the more dire. "I... I haven't the words," he said, lower lip trembling.

The Chief Inspector wasn't having it. "What happened to you in there, Jenkins? Report!" He let the back of his hand fly, figuratively of course. He consciously made a point not to let his actions run amuck through verbiage. "Report!" he demanded.

Jenkins stammered. "A mothers fondness found held weak fraternal!" he screamed. "No! No! I haven't the words!"

"My god!" Strunk screamed. "Her Dadaism! It's consuming him."

"Don't say another word," White said.

The Chief Inspector wasn't having it. Another of one of his men wasn't losing himself in Stein's madness. "Report, Jenkins!" he demanded, grabbing Jenkins by the collar and shaking him. "You're my agent, you understand me? You're on my time and my men have their heads together! If you lose yourself to this modernist then you're fired! You hear me? Out the door and straight to a career of tutoring and running contestant registration desks at beginner level spelling bees. Now pull yourself together and report!"

Fireworks fizzled in Jenkins' eyes every time The Chief Inspector slammed him into the wall. Trying to see over his sudden veil of tears, Jenkins' trembling hand found his holster and removed his red paintbrush. His lip trembled from fear of uttering another bit of nonsense, and the fear extended into his hand as he took his red quill to the wall and drew a multicolored spiral.

"What is it, Jenkins?" The Chief Inspector released the rookie and let him continue. "A snail shell? Some sort of vortex?"

Jenkins drew a vertical line down from the spiral.

"A lollipop?" White asked.

Jenkins nodded. He then drew a one armed stick figure with an X and an O for eyes, the lollipop protruding from one of them. Two smaller stick figures were looking on, with wide circles for mouths and eyes. A third one next to them was drawn with two dots for eyes and a horizontal line for a mouth.

"So," Strunk studied the crude drawing. "Are those the three wise men?" he asked, to which Jenkins shook his head. Strunk said, "Then they must be George Washington, Nikola Tesla, and I can only assume the unimpressed one is Edgar Allen Poe. He seems to be at about the turning point of his career. Together they three watched the fourth man be lobotomized by a lollipop. Him I do not recognize."

Jenkins pointed to Strunk with his red highlighter and nodded, tears flowing from his face. He turned back and drew an anchor over the lollipop.

"My word," Strunk said.

And then some sharp wit went over Jenkins' head.

Chapter 4:
Lydia

The marigold often doted over the bee that pollinated it. It had been a warm, late summer day. The marigold stood alone in its pot, as it always did. Several other marigolds were in their pots beside it, but it was entirely oblivious to them. It registered that the window had been opened, a difference understood only as that sometimes the air tasted different and sometimes it sifted through the flower's petals. The vibrations of a woman's steps and her voice typically signified the window was about to be opened or closed. The marigold couldn't understand a word, but found her tone soothing. It also knew the vibrations of her voice typically meant water, and for that the marigold grew rather attached.

The bee was something entirely unique. The marigold would never understand it for what it was, or even why. It knew him strictly through the feeling of delicate little touches. He moved its petals. He breathed. He snuggled into its softness for a long, lingering moment. And then just as the marigold felt it would last forever, the bee was gone.

From that day forth the marigold continued to know the warmth of the sun and stillness of night. It felt refreshed when it was watered and enjoyed the wind sifting between its petals. But whenever it heard the woman's voice and tasted the outdoor air, whenever the day was exactly like it had been, it always pined to feel those delicate little touches. Just one more time, it would think. Let it know those touches one more time.

T-Minus Six Minutes

The Chief Inspector, White, and Strunk all stared in horror as Jenkins stumbled forward, staring at the half of his red pen that was still in his hand, bleeding ink down his arm and soaking into his uniform. "My father gave me that pen," he uttered. He then looked down at the plot hole in his own chest, pierced straight through by a trailing preposition. As it retracted back through him, he coughed up his own red ink and permanently spattered corrections all over the floor. Jenkins fell to the bottom of the paragraph and the remaining three men saw an anagram for *scariest thing ever* standing over his corpse.

"A chest terse virgin," Stein's voice echoed through the halls. "Creativeness girth. Reteaches striving."

"What in the blazes?" White gasped.

Strunk stumbled away from the beast of sorts. "What is that thing?"

Stein chuckled, "Chatterers given tits."

The thing drooled horror story clichés from its razor teeth. Its spine arched with genre defying paradigm shifts, extending into a run on sentence tail that whipped back and forth in iambic tetrameter and concluded on the preposition stinger it'd skewered Jenkins with. It stood on two heavy-handed footnotes for the same word[21],[22]. Its black gold, boneless rib chest of oxymorons breathed icy hot with chaotic organization. The phrasing of its extended hands, reaching for the grammar police, ended in verbose clauses. And although the creature had no eyes, it could see the team of men through their imagination.

The Chief Inspector was the first to act, splashing the beast with half a bottle of white out. It screamed and hissed alliteration but didn't slow down.

"I fear we can't correct this, sir," Strunk said, backing away "It's just too much bad grammar! We have to retreat!"

"It killed Jenkins," The Chief Inspector said. As the thing pounced, he drew a red line across its wrist, but for the effort he was knocked across the room and into the wall. The man still landed on his feet and started to charge.

---

[21] The left foot was made of descriptions for *teeth* pulled straight out of bad teenage vampire romance novels.

[22] The right foot was made of all the things feet are described as doing in your grandmother's smutty grocery store sex novels.

Stein's voice echoed through the hall. "A chestier vet grins." The thing screeched at The Chief Inspector and pounced over him, a shrill of bad verbiage spewing from its lips. It raised its preposition over its head.

White glanced to Strunk. "Get him out of here!" he screamed, dashing at the thing.

"What are you doing?" Strunk yelled.

"Just being another literary device!" White tackled the thing just before the preposition could claim The Chief Inspector. "It's a mouthful," White said as the thing scrambled to buck him off. "Get the Chief out of here! Get him to Stein! I'll show this little first draft how to be copy edited. It's about to be whited out!" He then bit down on the scruff of the proverbial thing's neck.

Stein applauded. "A heretic's rev sting!" she laughed.

As Strunk pulled The Chief Inspector to his feet, they watched as White flailed about the room with the thing in his mouth. It bashed him into walls and off the ceiling. It rolled and tumbled. And in the flurry of chaotic grammar, two red pencils extended from under White's sleeves. He plunged them into the beast. It screamed and writhed, but White's bite was firm.

"Keep the bad words behind your tongue," White thought. "Keep them from ever coming out."

"We have to save him," The Chief Inspector ordered.

"No, sir!" Strunk snapped back, the only man to ever defy his superior. "We have to stop Stein! It's the only way."

The Chief glared at White flailing about the room, smashing through lamps and furniture, being rammed into Jenkins' corpse. He kept the thing in his mouth, but for how long? "Right," he said. "Right, let's go!" He then looked back to White, flopping and fighting on the floor, so much more than a literary device. He was far more a man than he'd been just fifteen pages ago. "Keep fighting, White!" he screamed. "We'll end this madness! We'll end it once and for all!"

Part 13.
The thirteenth part.

Billy Strunk was one and a half and sole heir to the family throne. Standing unsteadily in a hand-me-down bow tie and secondhand, patchwork suit, he played the first game his Daddy taught him. Wall. It was a simple game, but Daddy's favorite. And if Billy played it well he got a cookie. It was so easy. All the boy had to do was keep himself still against the blotchy red plywood. "I wish your mommy could see this," Daddy said, throwing a knife underhand. The blade stuck the plywood next to Billy's leg and the child bounced, clapping his hands and smiling. "Now don't you move, son. This next one's done blindfolded." Daddy waved around his handkerchief and playing peek-a-boo. "One day, you'll understand. Three generations your family's run this rodeo. Three generations and you'll be the fourth. Your grampy threw knives at Daddy. His daddy threw knives at him." He tied the handkerchief over his own face and stuck out his tongue, making Billy laugh and coo. "That's right, son. Keep making noise. Sister Elsie didn't make noise. Neither did brother Creighton." Daddy spun a knife in his hand and dropped it. Hushing a curse he took another blade from its sheath. "Sister Lola, she made noise. But she kept moving. You're not moving, Billy, are you?" Billy clapped. "Good boy," Daddy said. "Good boy." He raised the knife over his shoulder. He slowly went through the motion of his throw. "Your grampy said I should stick to the business side. After what happened to Grammy and all. But we're finally gonna show him, ain't we?" He threw the knife and heard it stick. "Ain't we, Billy?"

Chat Purr Foyer

The mansion itself wasn't at all concerned over the drama between the grammar police and Getrude Stein. Nor did it care that as matters escalated the entire world around this story was being ripped asunder into fragmented sentences, malapropisms, misused semicolons, and teen magazine articles. In fact, the only thing on the mansion's mind for the duration of these fake events was that somebody from another story you'd previously read had made a bagel with cream cheese in its kitchen. But just as the character was about to enjoy his or her breakfast, the phone rang, leading onto some amazing chain of events. All the while, the bagel has been sitting there; on the mansion's kitchen counter. Going stale. The cheese was surely bad at this point. Even though you just imagined it being made, freshness within the time of fiction is abstract. It could've been there for days now. Uneaten. Moldy. Just sitting there. On the counter. Why couldn't that character have taken it along? Why not eat it before getting to the really exciting story? All of that stuff was about to happen on an empty stomach. And all the while this bagel just sat there. And sat there. And sat there. And sat there. In the mansion. Aging in a spread of cream cheese. Silently. Just being. Even though it didn't exist. Nor did the mansion for that matter, at least not beyond the word for it. But there it was, now, then, and always. A bagel.

A Centre in a Table

The Chief Inspector and Strunk didn't find themselves locked in a small room, San Francisco, and The Rain Forest, staring intently at the light coming through the threshold of the closet door they'd just locked. But there they were. Shadows of noun words dripped in passing until the floorboards, city streets, and ancient dirt paths smoothed and settled.

"She's not declared a ransom," Strunk whispered over the silence. "No demands nor requests. What do you suppose she wants, sir? What's it all about? Cultural currency? Her place in college lit classes? A film biography in which she's portrayed through an award winning performance? Why are we running around this madness if not to satisfy some need?"

Several capybaras trotted by The Golden Gate Bridge and knocked over a broom and dustpan. The Chief Inspector watched as chain boats puttered along the Amazon floor crack of San Francisco Bay. He said, "I hate to speculate. The devil is in the subtext. We could spend all day tromping circles around the why of Stein and not arrive a single step closer in determining her end game. Do I believe she has an aim or some goal? Yes. It could be as simple as you say; validation for achievements. All people dream to know their place in the stars. Or rather the importance of such a place. That she brought us here, that it's her creativity driving this bungled tale to its ultimate conclusion no doubt solidifies some statement or another."

Strunk shook his head. He kicked over a bottle of all purpose cleaner, and in doing so uprooted several walking palm trees at 555 California Street. "But what statement? Where is the power in defiling structure? What did White and Jenkins have to die for? Rising action? Maybe some demented form of humor in Jenkins' case?"

The Chief Inspector's steel gaze fell over Strunk. "Reality is slipping away and we're being attacked by the very language we've come to correct. If there's a reason for this disaster it's been yanked straight from the discarded brain matter of a lobotomized ninth grade creative writing class drop out. I fear no matter how we view our circumstances we'll have them all wrong."

Strunk felt tense as The Chief Inspector watched him. Morning, midday, and a dull, flickering bulb all reflected through his eyes. Between all the lights, Strunk could see a reflection of himself in his commanding officer's left pupil. "View *our* circumstances," he whispered. "Sir, you're absolutely correct. This is cubist. We've been looking at it all wrong."

The Chief Inspector saw a smirk grow over Strunk's face. "All right," he said. "But before we go any further, I should tell you you're standing in an Alcatraz feces puddle."

They both looked down at Strunk's feet. After a considerable moment Strunk asked, "Is the feces part of the rain forest or closet setting?"

"Chicken or the egg, Strunk. Is it the chicken or the egg?"

Chapter Luck of Godot

ACT I
SCENE I. A forest

Enter ANGUS followed by BANDIT.

ANGUS

Nay and no, sir!
I aim not away but merely sideward.
If it vexes I should angle my station
through this woodland endeavor I of course offer
only my regret bejeweled apologies.
For I thought not to offend,
nor to misguide, certainly not to flee,
and to my utmost not to discover features which you
so sternly instructed are to remain secret.
My action was agreeably not clever but rather anxious.
The farmer oft toil over uncultivated lands
as the nun doth pray more fervently
should she stumble herself upon a brothel.
To the tip of your arrow I find myself no less acute.
But if your desire stands that I should remain as your Polaris
and not waver as the moon I with diamond clarity do understand.
But to this point may I inquire
as to the manufacturer of your crossbow?
Be the weapon of Danish, German, or even Eastern descent?
Could you speak with approbation to its oak-ness?
For I doubt not the sturdiness of your arm nor finger.
My travel companion's now deeply tunneled eardrum
may testify to the many seasons
in which the fruit of your skill hath ripened.
But to my fancy it strikes not uncommon
even a distinguished gentleman of your profession
may acquire his arsenal through less reputable vendors, perhaps.
I speak not to belittle but merely to express
the typical depiction of the roguish type
as painted to those fenced within the boundaries of law.
Not exclusively mind you.
As it was my darling wife, Helena,
lost her second eldest brother

to the accidental twain of such a contraption
as the one you so sturdily poise upon the aft of my beating heart.
The absolute stern, mind you.
Only the stern, as clearly the sight of my port and starboard
ripples you and I wish our waters placid.
But pray thee, if I am not to bend even in the slightest
from our forward trajectory may I
at least rest in the blanket of knowing
your crossbow was not forged by a Frenchman?
Should my two daughters, Hero and Luce,
lose their father well before his winter,
I'd like him not slain in the same manner as their uncle.
Treachery from a bandit lofts a certain romance
over the malfunction of a taut string and bolt.
Speak not further of their future mistrust of crossbows.
Although Helena raises them as ladies I possess little
doubt He may challenge my girls to the necessities of survival.
Should cross events transpire
calling upon them to throttle at the grips of crossbows
I merely ask we ensure they do not come to doubt
the functionality of the tools at their disposal.
Think upon my daughters, sir.
Allow me to let them know
the weapon operates strictly as advertised.
And with that matter settled, we may journey forth
with no future misunderstandings betwixt us.
For I shall remain steadfast in your employ, a loyal hostage.
You, an opportunistic adventurer, most shrouded.
I shall concern myself only in carrying
these gold sacks, your rightful possessions
with myself merely the vessel of their transport.
You concern yourself only in man's own fallible
requirement of occasional slumber. But trouble not over me again.
By crest and kin I am weightier than a bird
and won't take flight.
Genuinely, I am merry to assist in this
capitalistic little venture you've bestowed upon me.
For I grew bored last evening stewing about my campsite.
My cargo constituted mere luxuries for my abode.
The purse was meant to breathe
and I may make substitute purchase upon its next inhale.
My travel companion was but a lug hired to lug.
He was of no personal consequence and to the ranchers
I'm certain most easily replaced.
Betwixt us and the trees, he fares better left as food for the wolves.
So as you swift as the fox may deduce,

I view our encounter as a delightful diversion
through seldom travelled countryside. Nothing
more than a tale to rouse dinner guests over in coming Sundays.
The depiction of yourself will fluctuate greatly
in every merry telling, mind you. For I know not the face
of my captor and per his command
it leaves me only in the company of noncommittal imagination.
But perhaps you fancy yourself portrayed in a particular fashion?
Shall your height be doubled? Do you wish
me to speak of your barbarian arms
or perhaps with demon fires ablaze beneath your eyes?
Speak now. Tell me of the legend I'll boast of once you set me free!

ANGUS takes bolt from crossbow and stabs BANDIT.

ANGUS

Your eyes do tremor, sir.
The only demon revealed within crouches now,
a reflection of no other than my true self
aiding to soften your fall.
Do fight the blood you drown in.
For whatever oblivion awaits
a pestering pup who attacks a bear
is but two steps beyond the horizon.
Should this be your finale I wish you to squeeze
every drop and celebrate in that
you're still given the grace to suffer.
Although the book on life's great lessons close
many half read chapters early, should this
thin veil be wrenched aside and the thickness
of eternity be revealed I offer you some parting words.
The crossbow makes but a bandit.
Tis the close blade that forges a man.
Rest now, pup.
Leave this fool to his fancy untruths and rest.

BANDIT dies

Deleted Scene 27:
Well-lined pockets

She didn't say much but spoke best with her chainsaw.
Tripping on acid and her shoelace, Lunie gave her father a mouthful
that settled everything. The parts of him may gargle and shiver a minute
more, but none could refute her conviction. He said his piece. She left
him in parts. After the divorce and every bad Christmas present, but
more especially for his confession that she was a fourth generation
clone of his mother that he'd been experimenting on for the past sixteen
years, she was done.

Sighing at the bloodied mantle, she cut the power and let the
motor choke itself to sleep. She needed to breathe. Too much was
making sense. In this familiar place, she stood on new ground.
Suddenly she understood the electrodes that monitored her dreams. The
mazes, the steroids, and that time she'd been suspended from a plane by
a heart monitor all became too clear. Was she human or something less?
More of a monster, people might argue. Lunie sat in the recliner and
glanced at the coffee table. Half a cigarette rested on the lip of an
ashtray angled like an invitation. It wasn't until she started looking
about the room for a lighter that she remembered the news camera.
Something in the back of her head told her that the live interview had
taken a turn for the worst.

The Chief Inspector's name is not Gertrude Stein.

Chapter 16

"Darling? My darling? Is that you? Why did you never come home?"

"We can control this, sir!" Strunk screamed over the howling winds, holding a radio antenna lassoed to a golf club which was taped to an asparagus (sliced down the middle and folded so that its entire exterior could be seen through Cubist eyes) and suspended by a kite catching wave after wave of gaseous words expelling from an opaque carafe. Far, far below was an endless abyss of words swirling, churning, bubbling over each other.

"Strunk!" The Chief Inspector screamed back, barely able to hear himself. He clung to the edge of a cliffhanger, looking down at the typhoon of jumbled nonsense. "Strunk! This is madness! I don't understand what you're attempting! I doubt you understand what you're attempting!"

"I don't!" he laughed. "That's the point! The point of this all! Our actions and perceptions, the way we see and interact through the world as defined by the confines of language! Our grasp on reality is impaired only by the barriers we cross-communicate with! There is no English! There is no natural limitation on perception. Just the one we impose on ourselves! A complicated series of idioms and dialects similar enough to trick us into believing we can identify with one another's shared experiences! But the barriers we erect are made of the very tools we use to overcome them!" He cackled, randomly tossing assorted nouns into a vortex of adverbs. "It's cubism, sir! It's every angle all at once. Gertrude Stein isn't destroying the world through bad grammar! She's unfolding it!"

"You're using far too many exclamation points for this exposition," The Chief Inspector warned over the winds of change. "You're dribbling fantastical nonsense. Remember your station. You're an officer of the grammar police, sworn on Merriam-Webster to uphold structure, meaning, and syntax. Language is no more a barrier than my red pencil is a flounder. From the first two souls who agreed to call apples *apples* to the dying utterance of the last man alive, language is the defining utility of our existence and I'll be damned to see it ripped asunder by the careless whim of artistic hubris!"

"You have to trust me sir!" Strunk leaned further over the ledge, teetering at the cusp of falling action. "I'm in my element! There's still time! I can find him! I can still save White!"

"I'll trust you when you stop hunting for over-simplified explanations!"

"Sir," Strunk paused long enough to look over his shoulder, to stare up into The Chief Inspector's steel gaze one final time. The wind softened words drifted softly to sleep. Away. Away. Away. "Find the Cubist. I'll see you on the other side." Then he let go.

The Chief Inspector screamed, reaching out for his officer but couldn't grasp the ethereal concept Strunk had thrown himself into.

Strunk smirked as The Chief Inspector shrunk further and further away. He closed his eyes, spreading his arms as he descended through all the written scientific journals, medical textbooks, and jargon. He fell through want ads, user manuals, journals, and scripts. Not just in English but every language living, then dead. He felt every description of the air from every story and poem ever written rush by him and whip his hair. Magazine articles and newspapers fluttered, circling above him as he descended through mythology, countless diaries, and every early draft of the Dead Sea Scrolls. Hieroglyphics plumed as he passed. Just then, just as he saw every word ever used all at once, he shattered through the stale cream cheese of some old bagel and broke his spine against the first cave drawing of two stick figures chasing a rabbit.

The white hunter is nearly crazy. The difference is spreading.

Chapter Belly

Steam the wrinkles.
A clean slate is never born.
Will it jizz or drizzle?
Assign the belly lift spanked
So kind sleep runs
the gambit until bending back.
A belly lift eases somber.
When the statue costs a rock
statues spend the world.
A chip two chips three.
In every hand a chisel
steam away the wrinkles.
Mind to paper.
Paper to mind.
Bloody cuts slash and chisel.
Printed and pressed.
A swan eaten costs only the duck.
Broken egg.
 A broken egg.

Standing before you is a man
Buried in white wash,
Wrinkle free rank
steady and linear as the clock
locked in circles
ticking
ticking
ticking forward.
A belly seized
A clean slate born without a story.
He lost the chisels
that may have softened his edges.
Every correction thereafter made
A cut through pure creation.
He lost his chaos.
A clean slate lives as a corpse alone.
A clean slate always dies
full of steam.

Introduction

"Little wings pitter patter patter. The moth circles spins the nearer the light. Closer so close the wings patter." Gertrude Stein descended her own words as she lowered herself down to The Chief Inspector's level. She slyly smiled at his steel gaze and said, "The moth is drivers forward accretion for the light. Not for the glow. Not for the world revealed clarity. Why?" She paused on the word pause, taking in The Chief Inspector with a wink before joining him on a blank page. "Warmth. Not the light not the light not the touch but the feeling of the light."

The Chief Inspector wasn't having it. After multiple officers had gone mad, the deaths of Strunk and White, and that awful poem, he was done. "Gertrude Stein," he said with all the authority his office gave him. "You're under arrest for multiple counts of linguistic malarkey, grand theft language, misuse of the classical paradigm, inflicting mass hysteria with unlicensed cubism, ending the world, and murder."

"Flitter fritter words and flitter," Stein smiled. "Do you need a psychiatrist, dad for a funeral married since chapter four lollipop lollygag pops."

"Enough of your psycho babble." The Chief Inspector grabbed Stein by the wrist and tried to place his cuffs on her. But just as the bracelet touched her wrist, it became a cufflink. Stein laughed. Her wrist passed effortlessly through his gripping fingers. He stood agape. "What have you done?"

"Stock character, two traits," Stein smiled. "A widower overworked. Not meaty enough to bite. Sometimes there's a man flittering in the heard head of words resembled. Exclamation point."

The Chief Inspector reached for Stein again, throwing his full weight into her, but he passed straight through and fell onto the page.

She stood over him and shrugged. "My darling, there was never a home. There was never a man. Your fiction breathes nonsense words of an order made ordered the linear chosen. This is was will again be a performance painting but never the story. What exists but not is never was made?" The man looked up to Stein, her satisfied little smirk on her face and a tornado of words pluming behind her. He reached for his holster, his fingertips grazing the edges of his revolver, but not coming to grips until they found his red pen. "There is no there there," she said, reaching out to help him up. "Oblivion is in the space between. The devil is in the subtext. A man forced into knots can't untangle himself when rigid."

"Right," he said. "On that we agree." He then turned from Stein and stabbed his pen through the page.

Chapter 5

Professor Jenkins smiled, looking out from his desk at all his little students. Tiny heads and an assortment of crayons were scattered throughout the room. There was a little chatter, but nothing unruly. "How are your pictures coming along?" he asked. "Who wants to show theirs to the class?"

Several hands went up.

"Okay," he smiled. "How about you, Marcus?"

A little boy stood and held up his picture.

"Bring it to the front of the room," Jenkins said. "So everybody can see." Marcus nodded and shuffled around his chair, nearly tripping. As he made his way between the desks, Jenkins said, "Now then, tell us about your picture of *knowledge*."

Marcus held up a crayon drawing of a building. "I drew the South Library," he said. "And it has these roman pillars holding it up because knowledge makes you strong. And there's a Ferrari in the parking lot because smarter people can get better things."

"Excellent work," Jenkins said. "And how about you... Gerdy? What did you draw?"

"I don't want to," she said. "Mine's not as good as his."

"It's all right," Jenkins said. "No one piece of art is better than another."

The girl reluctantly pushed her chair back and walked to the front of the class. When she held it up, several of the other students giggled. She ignored them and said, "I'm not sure if knowledge looks like anything."

Jenkins leaned in his desk to better see her drawing. It was a series of scribbles and random shapes, crossing and crisscrossing into a rainbow of madness. "Very good," he smiled. "I think it's an excellent picture."

"Are you sure?" Gerdy asked.

"Of course," Jenkins said. "There's always something grand about coloring outside the lines."

About the Author

Keith Blenman lives in Metro Detroit, studies creative writing, and teaches forensic analysis. Should you ever happen upon him in your travels, please don't be offended by the lack of eye contact.

Acknowledgements

Thank you to the Estate of Gertrude Stein, Stanford Gann Jr., Georgia Glover, and Lauren Sawchuck for their permission to use Gertrude Stein's writing.

Thanks to Courtney Danyel for editing and trying to make sense of this abomination.

Thanks to my muse, Christina Irwin, for the "about the author" art, all your beta reading, and worlds of inspiration.

Thanks to Thomas Budday for all the critiques and constant feedback.

The "do you need a psychiatrist" scene was based on an idea from Mike Blenman. Thank you for letting me steal your brilliance.

Special thanks to Harry Campion, Caroline Maun, Maya Younis, Nathan Squires, Josh Blenman, Dan Blenman, Chris Blenman, Hannah Grimaldi, and all the kids at Tom & Campion's poetry group who critiqued much of this without knowing its context.

And of course thanks to Gertrude Stein for having written the original *Tender Buttons* in 1914.

Cover art by Midjourney

Other books by this author

Please visit your favorite ebook retailer to discover other fiction by Keith Blenman:

The Vecris
Whisper: A prelude to Necromantica
Necromantica
The Girl Drank Poison
Tales of Lythia

Roadside Attraction
Book One: Siren Night
Book Two: Tramp Stamp Vamp (coming soon)
Book Three: Ruff Stuff (coming slightly less soon)

Other fiction
Bartered Breath
Bonnie Before The Brain Implants
Braaaaaains
Entrees & Statistics
Tender Buttons Two: Disco Wrecklord
Where Dogs Sweat

Necromantica

The Kingdom of Fortia faces an apocalypse. Orcs have invaded from the East, massacring their way straight to the holy city Dromn. While the kingdom makes its final stand, a necromancer elf and her human companion plunge through the battle in a high stakes mission to loot the king's palace. But with the city aflame and the battle stretching to every horizon, can they pull of the greatest heist ever? Can they even escape with their lives?

Bonnie Before The Brain Implants
Exponential Innovations: Book One

Eponential Innovation's newest employee is Bonnie Neman; one of the greatest mind's the world will ever know, a recent college graduate, and therefore qualified only for an entry level position. As an introduction to this sci-fi comedy series, Bonnie tours several labs in new her workplace, repeatedly discovering just how easy it is to reach out and touch the impossible.

Roadside Attraction
Part One: Siren Night

Opening a monster series somewhere in the middle, Siren Night is a typical day in the life of Millie VanCastle. College drop out with telepathic abilities, as she drives her immortal, bigot boss, Gus, around the country, on the hunt for the biggest and baddest monsters of all time. When Gus picks up on the trail of bones left by a trio of sirens along the Gulf of Mexico, the hunt takes him to a karaoke bar in Alabama. Millie gets dragged along for a night of strong drinks, bad singing, guns blazing, blood orgies, and vampire skin boots that sparkle in the daylight.

Connect with Keith Blenman

I hope you enjoyed my book. I love to connect with fans, readers, and critics alike, so please check out my social media sites. Reviews on Goodreads, Amazon, iTunes, and other retailers are also always appreciated.

Twitter: @keithblenman

Instagram: @blenmankeith

Facebook.
http://www.facebook.com/keithblenmanwriter/

Subscribe to Keith's blog:
http://keithblenman.blogspot.com

www.ingramcontent.com/pod-product-compliance
Lightning Source LLC
Chambersburg PA
CBHW070650130626
46555CB00006B/2793